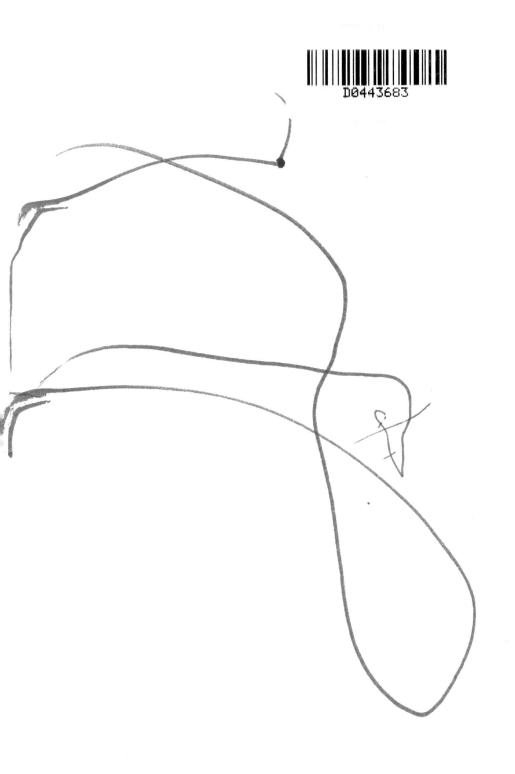

STARTING LINE READERS

Soccer
SCORE

BY CC JOVEN

ART BY ÀLEX LÓPEZ

WITHDRAWN

STONE ARCH BOOKS
a capstone imprint

Sports Illustrated Kids Starting Line Readers
is published by Stone Arch Books, a Capstone imprint
1710 Roe Crest Drive
North Mankato, Minnesota 56003
www.mycapstone.com

Library of Congress Cataloging-in-Publication data
is available on the Library of Congress website.

ISBN: 978-1-4965-4251-9 (library binding)
ISBN: 978-1-4965-4258-8 (paperback)
ISBN: 978-1-4965-4262-5 (eBook pdf)

Summary: Mia runs fast. Mia kicks hard.
But does Mia score a soccer goal?

Printed in the United States of America
010056S17

This is Mia.
Mia likes soccer.

Today is her first game.

Mia has new soccer socks.

Mia has new soccer shoes.

Mia has a new soccer shirt.

Mia has new shin guards.

Mia is ready!

Mia sees her team.
They warm up.

They stretch. They run.
They kick.

15

The game starts.

Mia runs fast.

Oh, no! Mia loses her shoe.

Mia kicks the ball with her other foot.

She misses the goal.

But her friend scores!

Goal!

Mia really likes soccer.

SOCCER
WORD LIST

game

goal

kick

run

shin guards

soccer

stretch

word count: 81